Goosebumps®

PRESENTS

Have you seen the new show on Fox Kids TV? It's creepy. It's spooky. It's funny. . . . It's GOOSEBUMPS!

Don't you love GOOSEBUMPS on TV? And if you do, then you'll love this book, *The Cuckoo Clock of Doom*. It's exactly what you see on TV— complete with pages and pages of color photos right from the show! It's spook-tacular!

So check under your bed, pull your covers up tight, and start to read *The Cuckoo Clock of Doom*. GOOSEBUMPS PRESENTS is so good . . . it's scary!

Look for more books
in the GOOSEBUMPS PRESENTS series:

Episode #1 *The Girl Who Cried Monster*
Episode #3 *Welcome to Camp Nightmare*

Goosebumps®

PRESENTS

THE CUCKOO CLOCK OF DOOM

Adapted by Carol Ellis
From the teleplay by Billy Brown & Dan Angel
Based on the novel by R.L. Stine

SCHOLASTIC INC.
New York Toronto London Auckland Sydney

A PARACHUTE PRESS BOOK

No part of this publication may be reproduced in whole or in part, or stored in a retrieval system, or transmitted in any form or by any means, electronic, mechanical, photocopying, recording, or otherwise, without written permission of the publisher. For information regarding permission, write to Scholastic Inc., 555 Broadway, New York, NY 10012.

ISBN 0-590-74587-5

12 11 10 9 8 7 6 5 4 3 2 1   6 7 8 9/9 0 1/0

Printed in the U.S.A.   40

First Scholastic printing, May 1996

It was an afternoon in fall — only a few days before my twelfth birthday. As I headed home from the park, I bounced my basketball. I listened to music on my Walkman. And I thought about my birthday.

I couldn't wait for my party. My mom had ordered a big chocolate ice-cream cake. All my friends were coming. It was going to be great.

There was just one problem — Tara, my little sister. Tara's five, and she's a real brat. But there was no way to keep her out of the party.

I kept walking and bouncing the basketball. Maybe Tara will get chicken pox or something, I thought. Then she'll have to stay in bed. I smiled and bounced the ball again. It was a bad bounce. The ball came down on a sprinkler and rolled under a hedge. As I bent down to pick it up, I got a weird feeling.

It felt as if someone were watching me.

Maybe somebody was hiding behind the hedge?

I ripped off my headset to listen for any strange sounds.

At first, all I heard was my heart thumping like crazy.

Then I heard something rustling behind the bushes. Maybe it's just the breeze blowing the dry leaves, I thought.

I heard the rustling sound again. "Who's there?" I asked.

Nobody answered.

I held my breath.

Then I heard it again. More rustling. Louder this time. And it wasn't dry leaves! Somebody was behind the hedge!

I reached down and quickly grabbed the

ball. That's when I noticed the drops on the sidewalk.

Red drops.

Bloody red drops.

A whole trail of them!

I glanced around. There was nobody in sight. I swallowed nervously and followed the trail of red drops. They led down the sidewalk and across the yard in front of my house.

Dead leaves crunched under my feet as I slowly walked across the yard. I saw more. A lot more. Then, up ahead, I spotted a big pile of leaves. And on top of the pile was a huge glob of blood!

I ran up to the leaf pile and stared at the blood.

Did somebody get hurt? What was going on?

I heard the rustling again. Something moved in the hedge behind me.

I had to find out what was back there. My heart pounded like a hammer. I took a deep breath. Then I grabbed hold of some branches and pulled them apart.

At that moment a bloody set of jaws clamped onto my arm.

"Aah!" I screamed in terror. A monster! I tried to pull away from the creature, but the bloody jaws wouldn't let go. I jerked my arm backward. It was covered with blood!

The jaws still wouldn't let go. I screamed and twisted really hard. I fell down and rolled against the pile of leaves. I scrambled to my knees. I had to get inside the house, or I'd be eaten alive! Just as I started to run, I heard someone laugh.

I stopped. I know that laugh, I thought. It isn't a monster.

I turned around slowly.

There she was. Tara. My skinny, bratty little sister. She held up a big plastic bottle of ketchup and laughed again.

"Gotcha, Michael!" she cried.

Ketchup, I thought. Not blood. Ketchup.

I glanced at my arm. One of Tara's hand

puppets was stuck to my sleeve. A ketchup-covered hand puppet.

I yanked the puppet off and threw it on the ground.

By then two of Tara's friends had crawled through the hedge. They stood there with Tara, laughing at me.

"What a krej!" Tara exclaimed to her friends. "I told you my brother was a krej!" She made a face at me. "That's 'jerk' spelled backward, Michael. You krej!"

This time Tara's friends laughed even harder. But I wasn't laughing.

"What's your problem, Tara?" I asked. "What did I ever do to you?"

Tara didn't answer. She took a step closer to me. Then she raised the ketchup bottle and squeezed it all over my face!

"That's it, Tara!" I yelled. I grabbed her and took away the ketchup bottle. "I've had it!"

Tara's friends ran off. She pulled away from me and ran toward the house.

"I'm going to get you, Tara!" I shouted.

"Mom!" Tara screamed. She was running for the back steps. I chased after her. I was furious! "I'm going to get you!" I yelled again.

Tara dashed up the steps. I was right behind her. She threw open the door. I raised the ketchup bottle and squeezed.

Whoosh! A thick spray of ketchup hit the door!

"Michael! Tara!" my mother cried. She hurried to the door. "What is going on?"

"Michael won't leave me alone!" Tara wept.

"What?" I yelled. "Tara's the one, Mom! She . . . "

"He's lying!" Tara shouted.

Then Mom saw what I was holding. "What are you doing with that ketchup?" she asked.

Then she looked at the door and frowned at me. "I want that cleaned up, Michael. Now!" She grabbed the ketchup bottle from me. Then she shut the door.

For a moment I just stood outside the

door, watching. Then I sighed and reached for the door handle.

The door wouldn't open. I yanked. It still wouldn't open. It was locked.

Tara's face suddenly peeked around the door. She gave me a sly smile.

"Gotcha again, you krej!" she whispered.

2

HAPPY BIRTHDAY MICHAEL! read the paper banner on the living-room wall. THE BIG TWELVE!

It was my birthday at last. All my friends were there. Josh and Henry. Mona, a girl I like a lot. And Mona's two friends, Ceecee and Rosie.

Tara was there, too. I tried to ignore her.

Everything was fine for a while. Then I started to open Mona's present. It was small and flat and wrapped in silver paper.

Josh stuffed a huge handful of chips into his mouth as I unwrapped the present. Josh is always hungry. "Wow, I wonder if it's a CD," he mumbled through the chips.

"I say it's a football," Henry squeaked. His voice was real high from sucking on helium balloons.

I finally ripped the paper off the present. It *was* a CD. "Awesome! Thanks, Mona," I told her, looking at the cover. "I don't have this one."

"You sure don't!" Tara interrupted, snickering. "You said that CD was stupid. You threw it out."

I felt my face start to get hot. Mona looked upset.

"But now Michael will probably like the music," Tara went on. "Now that he's in *love!*"

Everyone giggled. My face grew even hotter. Mona started twisting the ends of her brown hair. Josh burst out laughing. He laughed so hard that he choked and sprayed chips all over.

I wanted to strangle Tara. But there were too many people watching.

"Michael!" my mother called from the kitchen. "Can you give me a hand with the cake?"

I hurried out of the living room and into the kitchen. "Mom, Tara's ruining my party!" I moaned. "I don't want her there."

"She's your sister," Mom answered. She licked some frosting from her finger. "Your friends seem to find her very entertaining."

"But it's *my* birthday!" I protested.

Mom stuck the last candle in the cake. "Here. Take the cake. We'll light the candles, and you can make a wish."

I already did, I muttered to myself. But the wish didn't come true. Tara the Terrible is still here.

I picked up the cake and walked back to the living room.

"Oh, boy, cake! I'm starved!" Josh called out.

I glanced around. I didn't see Tara. Maybe my wish *had* come true.

I held the cake high and walked across the room. Everyone smiled at me. I grinned.

Then I saw a leg. A skinny leg, sticking out from under the table.

Tara's leg.

10

I tried to stop, but it was too late.

I tripped and went flying. So did the cake. It landed. Then I landed — *splat!* — right on top of it.

Everyone laughed.

"Hey, Michael!" said my friend Henry. "Aren't you supposed to serve your guests first?"

Everyone laughed again.

I wiped icing off my face and glared at my bratty little sister.

One of these days, I thought. Just wait, Tara. I'll get you one of these days!

3

Two days later the front doorbell rang. I opened the door. Two deliverymen stood on the porch. They held a big object covered in canvas.

"Delivery for Mr. Webster," one of the men said.

"Dad!" I called. "There's a package for you!"

Dad hurried to the front door. Mom and Tara came running from the kitchen. I opened the door all the way, and the deliverymen stepped inside.

"Oh, boy!" Dad cried when he saw the package. "It's finally here!"

"What is it, Dad?" Tara asked. "Is it for me?"

"No, it's for me," Dad answered.

Dad led the deliverymen to the den. Mom, Tara, and I followed. We watched as the men set the package against the wall. After they left, Dad rubbed his hands together in excitement. "I've been wanting this for a long, long time!" he told us. He pulled off the cover.

Underneath was an old clock. A black one with silver, gold, and blue designs painted on it. It had a bunch of knobs and dials and secret doors.

"It's ugly," Mom commented.

Dad smiled and rubbed the top of his bald head happily. "But it's magical."

"Magical?" I asked.

Dad polished one of the knobs with his sleeve. "That's what Anthony at the antique store said."

Mom rolled her eyes. "But can it vacuum?" she asked. "Does it polish furniture?"

I looked closer at the clock. "Cool. There's a dial that tells the year." I pointed toward the year dial.

"Don't touch it!" Dad warned.

I pulled my hand back. "What do you mean, the clock's magical?" I asked.

Dad hitched his pants up over his pot belly. "Well," he began in a low voice. "There's a story that the old man who built the clock lived deep in the Black Forest of Germany many, many years ago."

While Dad spoke, I stared at the clock. At its little doors. Its odd dials and knobs.

"The old man put a magic spell on it," Dad continued.

I bent closer to the clock.

Dad's voice dropped even lower. "But who-ever discovers the magic must beware."

Bong! Bong! Bong! The clock suddenly began to strike six. The small door on its face flew open. A fierce-looking yellow bird sprang out at me.

"Eeek!" I screamed. I jumped backward.

"Cuckoo! Cuckoo!" the bird chirped.

Tara shouted, "Michael said 'Eeek!' What a scaredy-cat! I'm going to tell everyone!"

I grabbed Tara. "You better not!"

"He's breaking my arm!" Tara whimpered.

"Michael, stop it!" Mom said.

I dropped Tara's arm. "How come I get blamed for everything around here?" I complained. I turned to Dad. Maybe he would understand. But he was busy with the clock.

"It seems to be working fine," he muttered. "Anthony said something was wrong with it. He wouldn't tell me what. But I can't find any problem."

Tara stood with Dad in front of the clock. She started fiddling with one of the knobs.

"Tara, stop that," Dad ordered. He looked at both of us. "I don't want either of you to put a finger on this clock," he told us in his most serious voice. "In fact, I don't even want you near it. Am I understood?"

Tara looked down at the floor. "Yes, Daddy," she whispered meekly.

No way can Tara keep her grubby hands off that clock, I thought. And I was right.

* * *

As I finished brushing my teeth that night, I heard a noise downstairs. It was coming from the den. I tiptoed to the landing and peeked down the stairs.

Tara stood in the den, right in front of the clock. She was playing with one of the knobs.

Should I tell Dad? I wondered. I didn't have to decide. Dad came into the den and caught my sister in the act.

"Tara!" Dad yelled. "I thought I told you not to touch that!" His voice grew louder. "If I find anything broken on that clock, you're in serious trouble!"

Serious trouble. I smiled and went to my bedroom. Now I had a way to get back at my bratty little sister!

I sat in bed and stayed awake until it was late. Soon, Tara, I thought with a smile. I'll get you soon!

Finally the clock in my room said seven minutes to midnight. I slipped out of bed. I opened the door and sneaked into the dark hall. I tiptoed across the landing to the stairs. Very quietly, I went down one step. Then another. And another. And —

"I love you!" a voice squeaked.

I froze in terror.

I slowly lifted my foot. I had stepped on one of Tara's talking dolls. She had left it on the stairs, as usual.

I stepped over the doll carefully and went down the rest of the stairs.

My heart raced as I sneaked into the den. Moonlight shone through the windows. Creepy shadows shifted in the room. I swallowed hard. But I forced myself to tiptoe toward the clock.

Whoosh! The curtain flew up. A window was open! I jumped a mile. My heart almost stopped. Then it started pounding harder than ever.

A huge gust of wind blew into the room. The open window rattled. I hurried over and quickly closed it. Then I held my breath and listened. The house was still quiet. I began to breathe again.

I turned to the clock. It looked spooky in the shadowy room. Almost alive. A shiver ran down my spine. I wanted to run. But I had to get even with Tara.

I tiptoed closer to the clock. The minute hand showed two minutes to midnight. Perfect. I kept my eyes glued to the clock and waited.

And waited.

Tick-tock. Tick-tock. The clock ticked on.

Eleven fifty-eight. Eleven fifty-nine. Finally the clock began to chime twelve o'clock.

Bong. Bong.

I waited for the little door on the face of the clock to open.

Bong. Bong.

Nothing happened. I leaned closer to the clock.

Bong. Bong.

The door still didn't open. Was something wrong? I leaned even closer.

"Cuckoo!" The door swung open. The ugly yellow bird sprang out in my face. I jumped back and lost my balance.

"Cuckoo!" the bird chirped again.

I fell to the floor. But I had to get that bird before it went back inside the clock.

"Cuckoo! Cuckoo!"

I scrambled to my feet. I reached and grabbed the bird by the head. One twist and the head was on backward.

"Cu-gaaa!" the bird croaked. "Cu-gaaa!"

I let go. The bird snapped back behind the little door.

Have fun explaining that, Tara! I thought with a smile.

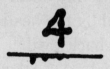

4

I couldn't wait to see Dad's face the next morning. When he found the twisted bird head, Tara would be in major trouble.

But when I got downstairs, my mouth dropped open. Dad stood on a ladder, hanging a banner. A banner that read HAPPY BIRTHDAY MICHAEL! THE BIG TWELVE!

"Why are you putting that up again?" I asked.

Dad glanced at me and frowned. "What do you mean *again*?"

Mom hurried into the living room. "What do you want for breakfast, birthday boy?"

"What's going on?" I asked. "My birthday was three days ago."

Tara trotted downstairs, yawning. When she saw the banner, she bragged, "I get to come to your party, Mike."

This has to be a joke, I thought. "Very funny," I told my family. Then I looked down and saw Tara untying my shoelace. "Cut it out!" I yelled at her.

"Michael, leave your sister alone," Mom snapped. "Tell me what you want for breakfast. Your guests will be here soon, and I have to go pick up your cake."

"Come on, you guys," I said. "The joke's over."

"What joke?" Dad asked.

I looked at Dad. Then at Mom. They weren't kidding. They both looked totally serious.

They really thought it was my birthday!

Two hours later, I was attending my twelfth birthday party. *Again!*

I picked up Mona's present just as Josh stuffed a handful of chips into his mouth. "Wow, I wonder if it's a CD," he mumbled.

"I say it's a football!" Henry chirped in his helium voice.

I unwrapped the present. "Awesome!" I heard myself say. "Thanks, Mona. I don't have this one."

"You sure don't!" Tara piped. "You said that CD was stupid and you threw it out!"

I dropped the CD. This was too weird! Everything that happened before was happening all over again! I backed away from my friends. Josh followed me.

"Josh, tell me the truth," I begged. "Weren't you here three days ago?"

He stuffed some M&M's into his mouth. "No," he mumbled. "Three days ago I was sick. I was barfing my guts out. My mom made me stay in bed."

"That can't be!" I cried.

"Michael, can you give me a hand with the cake?" Mom called from the kitchen.

I suddenly remembered tripping and falling with the cake. "Not this time!" I cried. My friends stared at me as if I were nuts. But I didn't care.

I turned and charged into the kitchen.

But she wasn't there this time. This time she was standing out on the porch. She held out the birthday cake to me. "Take this inside," my mom insisted. "We'll light the candles, and you can make a wish."

Before I knew it, I was heading into the living room. I started to open the screen door. Slowly.

"Oh, boy, cake! I'm starved," Josh called out.

Wait a minute, I thought. Where's Tara?

No way would she trip me again. No way!

My eyes darted all around. No Tara. Good.

I opened the door and stepped into the living room.

I stopped and searched for Tara again. I didn't see her anywhere.

I took another step.

Then another.

I suddenly spotted my little sister hiding behind the door.

It was too late.

Tara stuck out her hand and tripped me.

The cake went flying. I landed on my back. *Splat!* The cake landed on me.

"Hey, Michael!" Henry said, laughing. "Aren't you supposed to serve your guests first?"

"I'm caught in a time warp!" I insisted. That night I tried to tell my parents what was going on.

"Enough, Michael. You've been talking about this all day," Dad said. He and Mom were in my room. They were trying to figure out what was wrong.

"But it's the truth!" I told them. "I know it's weird. But I really am caught in a time warp!"

Mom reached out and felt my forehead. "He doesn't *feel* warm," she said to Dad. "Maybe I should take his temperature anyway."

"I'm not sick!" I told her. "You don't understand. The problem is my birthday."

Dad patted me on the back. "Well, your

birthday's over now, Michael. I'm just sorry you didn't like it."

"I did like it," I said. "I just didn't like it *twice*."

Mom came at me with a thermometer. I pushed her hand away. "I'm not sick!" I cried again. "You have to believe me. I woke up, and it was three days ago!"

"Try going to sleep, dear," Mom suggested. "You'll feel better in the morning."

"Sure you will," Dad agreed. "Like I always say, tomorrow is another day."

"It better be!" I told them.

After Mom and Dad left, I lay in bed and tried to figure things out. Two birthday banners. Two parties. Two cakes in the face.

What was going on? And why didn't anybody believe me? How could I be the only one stuck in this weird time warp?

I twisted and turned in the dark. I threw off the covers. Then I pulled them up over my head.

No way could I go to sleep.

Finally, I slid out of bed and tiptoed downstairs. I stared at my shadow on the wall. It seemed huge. It followed me all the way down to the den. The door to the den was closed. When I opened the door, I couldn't believe my eyes.

The clock was moving! It was alive and moving. Moving toward *me*!

I turned and ran down the hallway. The hall grew longer with every step I took. What's going on? I wondered in horror. I was afraid to look back, but I had to. I had to find out if the clock was coming after me.

It was!

The cuckoo clock was chasing me on spindly little legs!

I finally reached a corner. I turned and ran — right into a dead end!

The clock ran after me. I backed into the corner. The clock came closer. The numbers and hands on the face were all twisted. The face looked almost like a human face — a mean, angry human face.

The hideous clock was right in front of me now. It leaned closer. I pressed myself deeper into the corner. But I couldn't get away.

I opened my mouth and started to scream.

The clock tilted toward me even more.

Then the little door on the clock sprang open.

Out flew the bird.

But the head on the bird was Tara's head!

My little sister's head bounced around on the spring. Her mouth twisted as she laughed at me. "Ha-ha! Ha-ha!"

I screamed. Tara's head wouldn't go away. It dangled in front of me, laughing wildly. "Ha-ha! Ha-ha!"

I screamed again — and this time I woke up. I was in a cold sweat.

A nightmare! I thought. A horrible nightmare. I wiped my forehead. I waited for my heartbeat to slow down.

"Michael!" Mom rushed into my bedroom in her bathrobe. "What's wrong, darling?" she asked. "Did you have a bad dream?"

I nodded. I wiped my forehead again.

"It was just a dream," Mom said in her understanding voice. "It wasn't real. Now go back to sleep. You'll feel better tomorrow morning." She glanced at the clock on my dresser. "Look at that. It's midnight. It already *is* tomorrow! Happy birthday, Mikey!"

My birthday? Why was Mom talking about my birthday again? And why was she calling me Mikey? I was way too old to be called Mikey.

Mom turned on my bedside lamp. I blinked and rubbed my eyes. And then I noticed something strange. Mom's face looked younger. And she was thinner than before.

Mom smiled. "Happy birthday, sweetie!" she said. "My big boy is now six years old!"

"Six!" I screeched. My voice sounded very high.

I threw back my blanket and looked at myself in horror. I was wearing cowboy pajamas. Cowboy pajamas with fringe on them!

I glanced around my room. My rock and basketball posters were gone. My hockey

I was on my way home from the park when I saw red drops all over the bushes. Bloody red drops.

"Gotcha, Michael!" cried my bratty little sister, Tara. She popped up from behind a bush and squirted me with ketchup. I couldn't believe I thought the ketchup was blood!

A couple of days later, I had a big party for my twelfth birthday. When I carried the cake in...

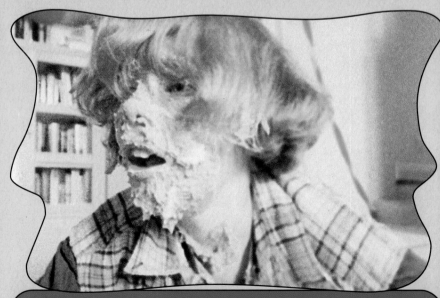

Tara stuck her skinny leg out and tripped me! The cake went *splat*—right on my face!

Two days later, my dad bought an old cuckoo clock. He said it was special and warned Tara not to touch it. Aha! I had a plan to get even with my horrible little sister.

At midnight that night I crept downstairs and turned the cuckoo's head around. Dad was sure to think Tara did it. That brat was going to be in big trouble now.

The next morning when I came downstairs, my parents were hanging my birthday banner—again.

"What's going on?" I asked. They said it was my birthday. I had no choice—I lived through my twelfth birthday once more.

"No!" I cried the next morning when I looked in the mirror. "It happened again. Time went backward." I was six years old!

And I suffered through my silly sixth birthday party again.

I ran away from my party to the antique store where my dad had bought the clock. I had to spin the cuckoo's head around to get things back to normal. But the door was locked!

That night my parents wanted me to go to sleep. No way! For me, good night could mean good-bye. I might disappear forever.

The next morning I was still here—but I was a baby! A little baby!

Luckily, Mom and Dad took me with them to the antique store. The clock was there! When nobody was looking, I started climbing toward the big clock...

The clock struck twelve. With my baby hand, I grabbed the cuckoo and spun its head around.

I was normal again! Everything was okay...until I discovered the magic of the clock!

league calendar was missing. The walls were covered with clown and dinosaur posters instead! A toy dinosaur sat at the end of my bed. A toy dinosaur that my grandmother gave me — when I was just a little kid!

I jumped out of bed and ran to the mirror.

A six-year-old stared back at me.

"No!" I cried. "It happened again. Time went backward again."

Dad hurried into my room. I stared at him in shock. He looked younger, too. His pot belly was gone. He wasn't bald.

"What's wrong, little buddy?" Dad asked.

I stared into the mirror again. "I can't be six," I cried in a little kid voice. "I'm *twelve*!"

"Mikey, you're six," Mom said flatly.

"I'm *twelve*!" I insisted.

"Honey, it's his birthday," Dad whispered to Mom. "Let him be twelve if he wants."

I wanted to scream. They didn't believe me. They didn't understand.

Then I thought of something. "Wait a minute!" I said. "If I'm six, where's Tara?"

Dad looked confused. "Tara? Who's Tara?" he asked.

Mom gave him a nudge. "Invisible friend," she whispered.

"Huh?" Dad looked confused. "He has an invisible friend?"

"Yes, and her name is Tara." Mom smiled at me as if I were a little kid. "Mikey, what does Tara look like?" she asked.

I couldn't believe what was happening. Was it a joke or another nightmare?

I ran out of my room and raced down the hall to Tara's room. I threw the door open and flipped on the light.

But it didn't look like Tara's room. It looked like an office instead. A desk sat where Tara's bed should have been. A filing cabinet stood where her dresser was. There were no toys. Books and papers sat on the shelves.

"Tara's gone!" I whispered to myself. "She has disappeared."

Mom and Dad caught up with me. "Michael, close my office door," Dad told me.

"It's time for you to get back into bed and go to sleep."

I didn't move. I was staring at the calendar on the office wall.

The calendar was for the year 1987.

"Time really is going backward!" I cried.

Dad laughed. "What an imagination."

"It's true. And I have a twelve-year-old mind stuck in a six-year-old body!" I moaned.

"I think we have a writer on our hands," Dad joked to Mom. "That would make a great science-fiction story, son. Time going backward."

Suddenly it hit me. "The cuckoo's head!" I cried. "When I turned it backward, I turned time backward. That must be it!"

I knew what I had to do. Somehow I had to turn the cuckoo's head back around. I ran downstairs. I heard Mom and Dad start after me. I couldn't let them stop me. I had to straighten the bird's head.

I raced into the den and pushed open the door.

"Oh, no!" I cried. Against the wall where the clock had stood was . . . nothing.

"It's gone!" I whispered in horror. "The clock is gone. And Tara's gone." What does that mean? I asked myself.

But I knew the answer.

The clock was gone.

Tara was gone.

Time was going backward.

And next — I would be gone.

5

As I stared at the empty wall, Mom and Dad rushed into the den. They both looked worried.

"It's gone!" I repeated. "The cuckoo clock is gone!"

"What cuckoo clock?" Dad asked. "We don't have a cuckoo clock."

"You're so stupid," I mumbled.

"Don't you call your father stupid!" Mom scolded me.

"Not him. Me. I'm the stupid one," I explained. "I should have known. Dad's not going to buy the clock for another six years."

Mom shook her head. "He must have a fever!" she said. It was clear that Dad agreed.

I was on my own. I had to turn time around by myself. The problem was how to do it without the clock. Then I remembered the antique store.

"Anthony's!" I shouted. "That's where the clock is! I have to go there!"

I started for the door. Dad stopped me and picked me up. "The only place you have to go is to bed, young man."

"Noooo!" I yelled. I kicked and screamed, but Dad held on tight and carried me back to my bedroom.

"Time to sleep, Mikey," Mom told me. "It's late."

"That's right," Dad agreed. "You'll be having your birthday party in a few hours. And the last thing we need is a grumpy birthday boy!"

HAPPY BIRTHDAY MICHAEL! read the party banner on the living room wall. THE BIG SIX!

Yes. I was six years old. And my friends were six years old. I sat at the table with them. Josh and Henry. Mona, Ceecee, and Rosie.

Everyone wore silly balloon animals on their heads. Everyone except me.

Everyone's face was smeared with cake and ice cream.

Every face except mine.

I couldn't eat. I didn't want food. All I wanted in the world was to be twelve again.

As I stared at the cake on my plate, Josh reached out for it. "You're not eating your piece, are you?" he asked.

I shook my head. Josh wolfed it down.

A man dressed as a clown leaned down next to my chair. Mom and Dad had hired him for the party. "Hey, birthday boy!" he cried. "I'll bet I can make you smile!"

He picked up some balloons and twisted them into the shape of an octopus. He waved the balloon-octopus in my face. I looked in the other direction.

I don't want to be six! I thought. I'm

twelve! And I have to get out of here. I have to get to the antique store and turn time around.

The clown twisted the balloon-octopus again. That twist gave it long, floppy ears. "How about a bunny, birthday boy?" the clown asked. He waved it at me. The floppy ears squeaked and hit me in the face.

The clown laughed.

There was a pin on the table for the pin-the-tail-on-the-piggy game. I stuck it in the bunny. *Pop!*

The clown backed away from me. "Well, my time is up," he said. "I've got to get to another party." He hurried out of the living room.

I slumped back in my chair.

"What's wrong, Michael?" Mona asked me.

"I have to get away," I told her. "I have to get downtown. To the antique store!"

Josh shoved a huge chunk of cake in his mouth. "What's an antique?" he tried to say with a mouthful of cake.

"Why do you have to go to the store?" Mona asked me.

"Because I'm getting younger by the day!"

She stared at me. "You just turned six, Michael. You're getting older, not younger."

"You don't understand!" I cried. "Today I'm six. But tomorrow, I might be . . . nothing!"

Henry laughed. "Hey, Michael! When you're nothing, can I have your presents?"

Henry was joking, but I couldn't laugh. I had a serious problem. I shoved back my chair. "You can have all my presents right now," I told Henry. "Just don't anybody tell my mom where I'm going!"

I jumped up and ran out of the room. I could hear Henry ripping open one of my presents, but I didn't care. I had to get to the antique store. I had to turn time around!

I raced out the front door and down the sidewalk. I didn't stop running until I reached town.

I glanced around. Broken-down houses and stores lined the street. Everyone towered over me. I was terrified. But I had to keep going and find Anthony's Antiques!

I passed an old building. The sound of rock music and crazy laughter was coming out of it. A tall man in a trench coat stood in the shadows.

"Hey, kid. Got the time?" the man growled. He stepped out of the shadows and blocked my way. I stared up at him. A huge scar ran down his face.

I shook my head. I stepped around him and began to walk faster. When I looked back, my heart skipped a beat. The scar-faced man was following me. "Come here. I want to talk to you," he called out.

I started to run across the street and almost crashed into a car. I reached the sidewalk on the other side and glanced back. The man was gone. I turned around.

Right in front of me stood Anthony's Antiques!

And in the window sat the cuckoo clock.

I sighed with relief. Then I saw the sign on the door: CLOSED FOR VACATION.

"Oh, no!" I screamed. I stomped my foot. I slammed my hand against the door. I rattled it. I yanked on the handle as hard as I could. The door didn't budge.

I had to do something! I had to get to the clock. I saw a brick and picked it up. I raised the brick above my head and . . .

A strong hand grabbed me from behind.

I froze in terror.

6

"Dad!" I cried.

"The kids at your party said you would be here," Dad told me. "What's the matter with you, Michael? How could you run away from your own birthday party like that? Your mother and I are very upset."

"I can explain, Dad — "

He cut me off. "And what are you doing with that brick?"

"Nothing." I dropped the brick. "Listen, Dad — "

He cut me off again. "What on earth is wrong with you?" he demanded. "Why did you come downtown alone? You know you're not allowed to do that. I'm very angry with you, Michael."

"I have to get to that clock in the window, Dad!" I told him. "It's very, very important! Do you know when the store will be open again?"

"I don't want to discuss it!" Dad snapped angrily. "I'm disappointed in you, Michael. And so is your mother. Now let's go home before she worries herself to death."

As Dad dragged me away, I glanced back at the clock. It seemed to be staring at me. Laughing at me.

I groaned. I had to get to the clock. Before it was too late!

That night I sat in bed in my cowboy pajamas. While Dad read me a story, I drew a picture with my crayons. First I drew a tombstone for myself. On it I wrote, *R.I.P. Michael Webster.* Under that I wrote, *1993 – 1981.*

Finally Dad came to the end of the story. "And he knew that if he ever needed it again, the magic baseball glove would be there, safe in the box in his closet," Dad read. He closed the book and yawned. "Okay, Michael," he said. "Lights out."

"Read me another. Please?" I begged. "Just one more. Please!"

Dad shook his head. "You were hardly listening. Besides, I'm tired."

Mom stuck her head into the room and spoke to Dad. "Is he still awake?"

Dad nodded. "He's afraid to go to sleep. He keeps talking about a time warp. And about disappearing."

"Michael, I want you to stop with this time-travel business," Mom insisted. "You are not going to disappear."

"Tara did," I told her.

Dad sighed. "And stop talking about this Tara! Who is Tara?"

Mom glanced at Dad. "Honey," she said, "if you read Michael one more book, maybe he'll calm down."

"I've been reading for two solid hours!" Dad cried.

"I know," Mom agreed. "But he's so upset. Maybe just a short book."

Dad shook his head firmly. "Absolutely not!"

"Mom. Dad. Don't argue about me," I told them. "It's not worth it. I'm not going to be here much longer, anyway."

Dad frowned. Mom felt my forehead. "He doesn't feel warm," she told Dad.

"Listen, buddy," my father said. "I'll turn on your night-light." He flipped on my special clown light.

Mom handed me my old, beat-up teddy bear with one missing eye. "Here, Mikey. Here's Mr. Grouchy Bear for my little man."

"Little is right. And I'm getting littler all the time!" I cried. I threw the bear on the bed.

Mom and Dad glanced at each other. They didn't have a clue about what was wrong.

"Try to go to sleep," Mom said, kissing me. "You'll be fine."

"No, I won't!" I insisted. "I'm not going to sleep. It's too dangerous!"

"Dangerous?" Dad repeated. "Don't be silly, Michael. Sleep is the best thing for you." He tucked me in. "Good night, son."

"Not good night," I told them. "Good-bye."

They left the room. The clock read ten-fifteen. No matter how late it was, I had to stay awake. If I went to sleep, I might never wake up. But my eyes felt like bricks. I held them open with my fingers.

I thought of the old cuckoo clock. The ugly yellow bird with its head on backward. I thought of my twelfth birthday party. And my sixth birthday party. And the tombstone I had drawn with my crayons.

But mostly I thought about the clock. It was ticking away in the store. Ticking time away. Ticking. Ticking. I squeezed my teddy bear and shivered with fear.

Tara's gone, I thought. And I'm next. Soon I'll be nothing.

I glanced at the clock again. Eleven fifty-eight.

Then everything went black.

7

The first thing I heard was birds chirping. I opened my eyes and glanced around. I saw cloud wallpaper. Above me a farm-animal mobile turned slowly. I glanced at my teddy bear. He looked brand-new, with two shiny eyes.

Then I saw the bars. Crib bars!

I crawled to the crib mirror and peered into it. What stared back at me was a little baby!

"Waaa!" I wailed. "Waaaa!" I sounded like a baby, too. I *was* a baby.

The door opened. Mom bent over my crib. She looked younger than ever.

I cried and sniffled. Then I smelled something.

"Uh-oh! Does Mikey need his diaper changed?" Mom asked.

"Waaaa!" I wailed.

Mom felt my forehead. "I hope you don't have a fever. Maybe I should take your temperature." She picked up a thermometer and dipped it in Vaseline.

I wailed even louder.

Dad walked in. "What's wrong with my little man?" He poked me in the belly and tried to make me laugh.

Mom checked the thermometer. "His temperature is normal."

Dad frowned. Then he smiled. "I have an idea! How would my little buddy like to go for a nice walk downtown?"

Downtown? Yes! I stopped crying in a flash. "Goo, goo. Goo, goo!" I gurgled happily.

"We can do a little window shopping," Dad said to Mom.

"Goo, goo!" I made happy sounds. I waved my fists in the air. I grinned.

Dad kept looking at Mom. "We could even take a look in that antique store."

What luck! I kicked my feet and bounced around the crib. "Goo, goo, goo!" I cried.

"You mean Anthony's Antiques?" Mom asked Dad. "I don't think so."

Oh, no! I thought. Mom's going to ruin everything. I stopped gurgling. I started to whimper.

"I like Anthony's," Dad told Mom. "What's wrong with it?"

I glanced at Mom, holding my breath.

"Anthony charges an arm and a leg," Mom said.

I whimpered again. Louder. My mom was being impossible.

She looked down at me. "Maybe we shouldn't go anywhere at all. Michael's getting very fussy."

I stopped whimpering. I didn't want to sound fussy. I waved my fists and grinned at Dad instead.

"Michael's fine," Dad insisted. "Come on, honey. Let's go to Anthony's. We'll just look, okay?"

I waited for Mom's answer.

"Well . . ." She sighed. "Okay. Let's go."

Yes! I would have another chance at the cuckoo clock. Probably my last chance!

Mom pushed the stroller downtown. Dad walked beside her. The neighborhood didn't look as shabby as before. It was younger, too.

I kept trying to say *cuckoo*. "Cugoo," I gurgled. "Cugoo."

"I think Mikey's trying to tell us something," Mom told Dad.

I was. "Cugoo!" I cried. "Cugoo!"

"He wants a cookie," Dad said.

Mom shoved an animal cracker in my mouth. I spit it out and started to cry.

When we turned a corner, I stopped crying. Anthony's Antiques stood just a few doors away! I pointed to it. I tried to say *let's go*. "Leh bo!" I cried.

"Yes. Baby clothes!" Mom said, misunderstanding me. She pointed to the store next to Anthony's. "I need some things for the baby. Why don't we go there instead?" she asked Dad.

No baby clothes! I needed the clock! "Mom-ma. Da-da," I stuttered. "Coogu!"

"Michael has plenty of baby clothes," Dad told Mom. "Let's go into Anthony's, the way we planned."

Good old Dad, I thought. "Leh bo!" I shouted.

Mom and Dad laughed. I don't know what they thought I was saying. Finally they wheeled me into Anthony's antique store.

Anthony rushed up to greet us. "Hello, Mr. Webster. Mrs. Webster." He bent down and smiled at me. "Hello, Mikey! How are you today?"

"Cugoo gock!" I gurgled. "Cugoo gock!"

Anthony laughed. He didn't understand me. He looked at Mom and Dad. "What can I show you two today?" he asked them.

"Gock!" I cried. "Cugoo gock!"

Dad stuck a cookie in my mouth to keep me quiet. "We'd like to take a look at that table in the window," he said to Anthony.

"Sure. Let's go," Anthony told him.

"How much is it?" Mom asked.

"Well, look at it first," Anthony said. "Then we'll talk money."

The three of them moved toward the window. I spit out the cookie and quickly looked around. Old furniture and dusty antiques stuffed the narrow aisles. I saw a strange bird mask. An ancient suit of armor. Chairs. Tables.

There it was! On top of one of the old tables, I finally saw the cuckoo clock. The hands said five minutes to twelve.

I glanced toward the window. Mom and Dad and Anthony were still there. I looked back to the clock.

Four minutes to twelve.

Not much time. I fumbled with the seat belt on my stroller. It was stuck!

I fumbled some more.

I finally pulled it loose at last and climbed out. Mom and Dad were still busy with Anthony. I couldn't walk, so I began to crawl down the aisle toward the clock.

Three minutes to twelve.

The clock was on the top of a table. I

crawled close to the table. The clock was too high up to reach. I glanced around. I saw a box on the floor near the table. An old rocking chair stood on top of the box. A baseball bat was wedged under the rockers. That meant the chair wouldn't wobble.

Two minutes to twelve.

I climbed carefully onto the box. Then up onto the rocking chair. So far, so good.

One minute to twelve.

I reached for the clock. Oh, no! The baseball bat started to roll out from underneath the chair. I wobbled, but I didn't fall. I reached for the clock again.

The bat rolled farther. I wobbled — and fell against the clock! But I grabbed the side of the clock and held on tight.

Bong! Bong! The clock began to strike twelve. I stared at it. Waiting. Waiting for the cuckoo.

At last the little clock door opened. I reached up to grab the cuckoo's head.

Instead of a bird, a toy woodsman marched out.

I had the wrong clock!

The rocking chair wobbled again. This time the bat rolled off the box and banged its way to the floor.

"What was that?" It was Dad's voice.

"Michael?" Mom cried. "Where's the baby?"

I turned around and looked down the aisle. Mom and Dad were running toward me. And right in front of me, I suddenly saw another clock.

A clock striking twelve — with an ugly yellow bird popping out of it.

The right clock! I could still turn time around!

I rocked backward, then forward in the rocking chair as hard as I could. I reached for the bird's head.

And missed.

"Grab that baby!" Anthony shouted.

"Michael!" Mom yelled.

"Cuckoo!" the yellow bird chirped.

It was my last chance. I rocked back. Then forward. Dad's hands reached for me.

I lunged for the bird. My arm knocked against the year dial, and — something fell off. I couldn't stop to look. I had to turn the bird's head around.

"Cu . . . " the bird cried. I grabbed the head. And twisted.

"Gaaaa!" it croaked.

Then came a blinding flash of light.

"Michael, how many times have I told you to stay away from that clock!" Dad was shouting.

I opened my eyes. I was in the den. My hand still held the yellow bird's head. Its beady eyes stared into mine. The head was turned the right way.

I let go of the bird. I staggered backward and bumped into Dad.

Dad frowned at me. Then he walked to the clock. I stared at him. His pot belly was back. He was bald again.

"You're twelve years old, Michael," Dad said to me. "Act like it."

Twelve years old?

I glanced down at myself. I was wearing jeans and a T-shirt. No more diapers. No more cowboy pajamas.

Dad was right. I *was* twelve years old again!

I did it, I thought. *I turned time around.*

I ran to Dad and hugged him. "I love you, Dad!" I cried.

"I love you, too," Dad told me. "But you have to keep your hands off my cuckoo."

"Lunch is ready," Mom announced from the doorway. She looked like her old self.

I ran over and kissed her. "I love you, Mom!" I cried. "And I'm starving. What are we having for lunch? I'll get Tara!"

Mom and Dad looked confused. "Who's Tara?" Mom asked.

"What do you mean?" I asked. "Tara, my little . . ."

I stopped talking. I dashed from the den and ran upstairs to Tara's room.

But it wasn't Tara's room. It was still an office. I couldn't believe it.

"Michael!" Dad called. "Come here!"

Uh-oh, I thought. What now? Slowly I went down to the den.

Dad looked up from the clock. "I think I found the flaw Anthony warned me about. See the year dial?"

I stared at the numbers on the dial. 1986, 1987, 1989.

"The year 1988 is missing," Dad said.

That must be what I knocked off, I thought.

"Nineteen eighty-eight!" I said in a choked voice. "That's the year Tara would have been born."

Dad frowned. "Who is this Tara?"

I started to tell him. Then I stopped. I even grinned. "Nobody, Dad," I said with a shrug. "Nobody."

Dad laughed. "You nut," he teased. "Let's go eat."

"I'll be right there," I said.

After Dad left, I turned to the clock. "So Tara the Terrible has never been born," I said quietly. "I suppose there's some way to go back in time and get her. Right?"

The clock ticked.

"I guess I ought to do that," I said. "And I will. Really."

The clock ticked.

"One of these days."

I grinned again.

"Maybe."

GET Goosebumps®

by R.L. Stine

☐ BAB45365-3	#1	Welcome to Dead House	$3.99
☐ BAB45366-1	#2	Stay Out of the Basement	$3.99
☐ BAB45367-X	#3	Monster Blood	$3.99
☐ BAB45368-8	#4	Say Cheese and Die!	$3.99
☐ BAB45369-6	#5	The Curse of the Mummy's Tomb	$3.99
☐ BAB45370-X	#6	Let's Get Invisible!	$3.99
☐ BAB46617-8	#7	Night of the Living Dummy	$3.99
☐ BAB46618-6	#8	The Girl Who Cried Monster	$3.99
☐ BAB46619-4	#9	Welcome to Camp Nightmare	$3.99
☐ BAB49445-7	#10	The Ghost Next Door	$3.99
☐ BAB49446-5	#11	The Haunted Mask	$3.99
☐ BAB49447-3	#12	Be Careful What You Wish for...	$3.99
☐ BAB49448-1	#13	Piano Lessons Can Be Murder	$3.99
☐ BAB49449-X	#14	The Werewolf of Fever Swamp	$3.99
☐ BAB49450-3	#15	You Can't Scare Me!	$3.99
☐ BAB47738-2	#16	One Day at HorrorLand	$3.99
☐ BAB47739-0	#17	Why I'm Afraid of Bees	$3.99
☐ BAB47740-4	#18	Monster Blood II	$3.99
☐ BAB47741-2	#19	Deep Trouble	$3.99
☐ BAB47742-0	#20	The Scarecrow Walks at Midnight	$3.99
☐ BAB47743-9	#21	Go Eat Worms!	$3.99
☐ BAB47744-7	#22	Ghost Beach	$3.99
☐ BAB47745-5	#23	Return of the Mummy	$3.99
☐ BAB48354-4	#24	Phantom of the Auditorium	$3.99
☐ BAB48355-2	#25	Attack of the Mutant	$3.99
☐ BAB48350-1	#26	My Hairiest Adventure	$3.99
☐ BAB48351-X	#27	A Night in Terror Tower	$3.99
☐ BAB48352-8	#28	The Cuckoo Clock of Doom	$3.99
☐ BAB48347-1	#29	Monster Blood III	$3.99
☐ BAB48348-X	#30	It Came from Beneath the Sink	$3.99
☐ BAB48349-8	#31	The Night of the Living Dummy II	$3.99
☐ BAB48344-7	#32	The Barking Ghost	$3.99
☐ BAB48345-5	#33	The Horror at Camp Jellyjam	$3.99
☐ BAB48346-3	#34	Revenge of the Lawn Gnomes	$3.99
☐ BAB48340-4	#35	A Shocker on Shock Street	$3.99
☐ BAB56873-6	#36	The Haunted Mask II	$3.99
☐ BAB56874-4	#37	The Headless Ghost	$3.99
☐ BAB56875-2	#38	The Abominable Snowman of Pasadena	$3.99

❑ BAB56876-0	#39	How I Got My Shrunken Head	$3.99
❑ BAB56877-9	#40	Night of the Living Dummy III	$3.99
❑ BAB56878-7	#41	Bad Hare Day	$3.99
❑ BAB56879-5	#42	Egg Monsters from Mars	$3.99
❑ BAB56880-9	#43	The Beast from the East	$3.99
❑ BAB56644-X		Goosebumps 1996 Calendar	$9.95
❑ BAB62836-4		Tales to Give You Goosebumps Book & Light Set Special Edition #1:	$11.95
❑ BAB26603-9		More Tales to Give You Goosebumps Book & Light Set Special Edition #2:	$11.95
❑ BAB73909-3		Even More Tales to Give You Goosebumps Book and Boxer Shorts Pack Special Edition #3	$14.99
❑ BAB55323-2		Give Yourself Goosebumps Book #1: Escape from the Carnival of Horrors	$3.99
❑ BAB56645-8		Give Yourself Goosebumps Book #2: Tick Tock, You're Dead	$3.99
❑ BAB56646-6		Give Yourself Goosebumps Book #3: Trapped in Bat Wing Hall	$3.99
❑ BAB67318-1		Give Yourself Goosebumps Book #4: The Deadly Experiments of Dr. Eeek	$3.99
❑ BAB67319-X		Give Yourself Goosebumps Book #5: Night in Werewolf Woods	$3.99
❑ BAB53770-9		The Goosebumps Monster Blood Pack	$11.95
❑ BAB50995-0		The Goosebumps Monster Edition #1	$12.95
❑ BAB60265-9		Goosebumps Official Collector's Caps Collecting Kit	$5.99
❑ BAB74586-7		Goosebumps Presents #1: The Girl Who Cried Monster	$3.99
❑ BAB74587-5		Goosebumps Presents #2: The Cuckoo Clock of Doom	$3.99

Scare me, thrill me, mail me GOOSEBUMPS now!

Available wherever you buy books, or use this order form. Scholastic Inc., P.O. Box 7502, 2931 East McCarty Street, Jefferson City, MO 65102

Please send me the books I have checked above. I am enclosing $_____ (please add $2.00 to cover shipping and handling). Send check or money order — no cash or C.O.D.s please.

Name _____Age _____

Address _____

City _____State/Zip _____

Please allow four to six weeks for delivery. Offer good in the U.S. only. Sorry, mail orders are not available to residents of Canada. Prices subject to change.

GB1095

Picture-Perfect Nightmare

Goosebumps®

Sourball. That's what Greg calls his English teacher, Mr. Saur—a real *grouch*. Old Sourball gave Greg a big fat "F" on his oral report just because he didn't believe Greg's story about a strange camera and the evil pictures that it took.

Poor Greg. Not only does he get a low grade, but now that the camera's around, bad things keep happening. Really bad things. Just like the first time....

Goosebumps #44
Say Cheese and Die—Again!
by R.L. Stine

Coming to a bookstore near you!

What could be better than ten new Goosebumps stories?

Goosebumps®

Ten new stories *and* awesome Curly boxer shorts

Can Jeff convince his parents there's a live mummy in the basement? Will Adam escape from a monstrous flying gargoyle? Is Brian's boarding school turning kids into robots?

You'll have all the answers <u>plus</u> your own Curly boxer shorts when you get:

Even More Tales to Give You Goosebumps Book & Boxer Shorts Pack
by R.L. Stine

Coming to a bookstore near you!